THE PATIO CLUB®

WRITTEN AND ILLUSTRATED BY

# CARYN MOTTILLA

# *Earl's Summer Surprises*

**Earl's Summer Surprises**

**The Patio Club** ®

Published by Open Window Publishing

Castle Rock, CO

Copyright © 2019 Caryn Mottilla. All rights reserved.

Publisher's Cataloging-in-Publication data

Names: Mottilla, Caryn, author.
Title: Earl's Summer Surprises / by Caryn Mottilla.
Description: First trade paperback original edition. Also available as an ebook. | Castle Rock [Colorado] : Open Window Publishing, 2019. | Series: The Patio Club.
Identifiers: ISBN 978-0-9997471-7-9
Subjects: LCSH: Old age—Fiction. | Month of May—Fiction. | Aging parents—Fiction. | Short stories.
BISAC: FICTION / General.
Classification: LCC PS374.O43 | DDC 813–dc22

Cover design by Caryn Mottilla

QUANTITY PURCHASES: Schools, companies, professional groups, clubs, and other organizations may qualify for special terms when ordering quantities of this title. For information, email ThePatioClub@gmail.com.

**OPEN WINDOW**
PUBLISHING

The Patio Club® is dedicated to the men and women in assisted living communities, memory and Hospice care who have listened to the adventures of The Patio Club®. They expressed their hope for these stories to be published and shared with others across the country.

# Introducing the Patio Club

The Patio Club was originally formed by two sets of sisters—Elaine and Adele from New Jersey, and Betty and Mildred from Kentucky. The women were young when they met in the 1940s. The years passed by, and later in life, the four adventurous women made a pact that after they died they would meet up and visit retirement and assisted living communities. After they passed away, they came to Happy Visions Retirement Home and liked it so much they decided to stay.

The women call themselves "The Patio Club," because they sit outside on the patio of Happy Visions. Each day, Elaine, Adele,

Betty and Mildred are surrounded by colorful sparkles, and they meet a steady stream of interesting visitors and residents who pass through Happy Visions on their way to unknown destinations.

One amazing thing is that the Patio Club can look to the sky and watch a video of each person's life. This precious gift lets the Patio Club understand the unique story that each person carries with them.

# Earl's Summer Surprises

THE SOFT LIGHT OF DAWN SLOWLY APPEARED on the eastern horizon. It was 4:45 a.m. A nearby nest of baby birds began chirping as they welcomed the approaching day.

Behind the bushes lining the patio, a tall man wearing a plaid wool cap stood next to his motorized scooter. Suddenly, the man took off his cap and tossed it onto the patio.

As the golden light of dawn appeared over the nearby mountains, Elaine, Adele, Betty and Mildred appeared

on the patio and sat on the festive cushions on the patio chairs. Lavender sparkles swirled around the women in the cool morning air.

As sunlight began to dance across the patio, Elaine noticed the wool cap on the patio tiles. "Look," said Elaine as she picked up the cap. "It looks like a man's plaid cap from Scotland. I should know because years ago, I visited Scotland with my travel group. Caps like these were everywhere. They are made in many different colors. Believe it or not, they are called 'bonnets,' but I don't believe men in the United States would wear them if they were called by that name!"

Elaine looked inside the cap and saw it was lined with satin. Stitched into the lining was a "Made in Scotland" label.

"This cap was made in Scotland!" exclaimed Elaine. "Judging from the condition of it, I would say it has been worn many times over the years.

"Oh, look!" Elaine continued. "Someone wrote the date 'October, 1996' in blue ink next to the label. I bet that's when they began wearing it.

The wool cap was gold, brown and red. Its colors looked similar to leaves that litter the ground in fall. As Elaine held the cap in her hand, she did not see a thin—almost invisible—string extending from the cap. The string was as fine as clear fishing line.

Elaine, turned to hand the cap to Adele. At the moment she did this, someone whistled from behind the bushes, just as the cap was ripped out of Elaine's hands. The women jumped from this unexpected surprise!

As the women watched, the cap continued sliding across the patio. They saw the string that was pulling the cap just as Earl came out from behind the bushes. Earl was laughing as he dusted off his wool cap and put it on his head.

"Come on, my whistling didn't scare you that much,

did it?" asked Earl.

The four women were surprised by Earl's sudden entrance. They could tell he was joking with them.

"My name is Earl. I saw you ladies enjoying the sunrise. It seemed like a good idea to give you a surprise to start your day."

Earl was tall with big hands, large glasses and strawberry blond hair. His smile revealed he had no remorse for surprising the women. In fact, he was enjoying himself!

"Are you crazy?" exclaimed Mildred. You could have scared us half to death!"

Adele laughed and said, "Wait a minute. We ARE dead!" Elaine, Betty and Mildred laughed at Adele's joke.

Earl was laughing as well. He said, "I arrived at Happy Visions a few weeks ago. Before that, I lived in Pennsylvania my entire life. Most people who knew me

said I was a 'real character.' There is no telling what they really meant by that description."

Earl continued speaking. "Honestly, I've always enjoyed surprising people. I couldn't resist tying a string to my cap and surprising you by pulling it out of your hands. You should have seen your reaction!"

Adele spoke slowly and asked Earl a question. "Has anyone ever passed out when you surprised them?"

Earl's blue eyes sparkled as he pondered Adele's question. He chuckled and answered, "Maybe a few people came close. However, I don't believe anyone ever passed out."

Earl noticed white clouds beginning to fill the blue sky. "I know you ladies call yourselves 'The Patio Club.' Rumor has it you can look to a video in the sky and learn something about me. Why don't you take a look now?"

This came as another surprise to the women. They didn't realize anyone knew of their special gift for watching

the sky's video of a person's life.

Betty found Earl very entertaining. She said, "That's a great idea, Earl. Let's see what the video has to say about you and about your life."

As the small group looked up, the video began to play. It showed a preacher standing in front of a room the day of Earl's funeral. The preacher said, "I have not known Earl very long, but I understand he was a real character. It seems his intentions were always to bring a smile—and sometimes controversy—to family and friends by surprising them. Does anyone have anything to share about Earl and how he touched their life?"

A small line quickly formed as one by one friends and family remembered Earl. The first to speak were Earl's grandsons. They spoke of Earl's love of nature. They remembered walks he took with them to a pond near where he lived.

Earl's two grandsons recalled the first surprise Earl

gave them. "Pap" as they called him, brought six colorful eggs for an Easter egg hunt. Earl hid the eggs and as quickly as Earl's grandsons found them, Earl would hide the eggs again. The children were sure they had found almost fifty eggs that day. Quite a few years passed before Earl's grandsons discovered that Earl kept hiding the same six eggs.

Friends spoke of Earl's service to his country during World War II and his love of family histories. "Earl had a good heart, and he enjoyed giving people his attention." A few people in the crowd sniffed when they heard this.

A distant cousin spoke next and said, "Earl always showed up unannounced wherever he went. He liked surprising people this way. No one ever threw him out—at least that I heard about. We used to joke and say Earl should have been named 'Early' because wherever he went, Earl was always early or completely unexpected!"

The women of the Patio Club were shocked by these revelations. When Earl saw their reactions, he chuckled

and said, "Why, you're not going to believe these people, are you? I can't believe they waited until the day of my funeral to talk about me this way!"

Earl laughed and said, "I surprised my sister and my wife's sister when we were first married. We invited them to lunch. I told each of them that the other sister was hard of hearing. I said they should yell to make sure they could be heard. Well, the day of the lunch when we introduced them, they started yelling at each other until they realized I had lied about their hearing. It was one of my favorite surprises! My sister and sister-in-law were only mad at me for a brief time!"

The video continued and suddenly went back to a time before Earl's funeral. Earl was sitting in his favorite brown chair in his living room reading the newspaper. His older son walked through the front door to pay Earl a visit after returning from a trip to Scotland.

The women watched as Earl's son surprised his dad by tossing him a brown paper bag. Earl's son was

astonished Earl had caught the bag. His son said, "Good catch, Dad! I brought you a surprise."

Earl unfolded the crunchy paper bag and reached inside. He pulled out the plaid wool cap from Scotland. Earl was delighted by this special gift! Before he put it on, he quickly took a pen and wrote the date in blue ink on the inside of his new cap. The date was October, 1996. Then Earl put on his prized Scottish cap and said, "I will wear this every day for the rest of my life. When I die, I am taking this with me!"

The video moved forward in time and showed Earl's recent arrival at Happy Visions. He wore his cap that first day as he drove his beloved motorized scooter. It had an American flag on a pole on the back of it. Earl spun his scooter in circles on the front lawn and waved to the residents like he was a movie star.

The video ended, and Earl quietly left the patio unnoticed by the women. All that remained in the space where he stood, was a cloud of red, white and blue sparkles

floating soundlessly in the summer air.

"I remember the day Earl arrived," said Adele. "Not too long after his first day here, people began talking about someone playing jokes on the residents. After what we have seen today, I think it's safe to say Earl is the one behind the unexpected surprises."

Betty thought for a moment and said, "I've often seen Earl speaking with residents. Several of them mentioned Earl's gift for remembering each person's name along with their complete family history!

"I know," said Adele. "People really like that about him. I've listened as he questioned people at great length about their families. Most of the time, he ends up knowing someone from their family tree—even though they lived in another state!"

The video came to life once more as people bid their final farewells to Earl the day of his funeral. Just as Earl had declared years earlier, he was buried along with his

prized Scottish cap. Earl's amazing life had lasted ninety-nine years and eight months.

Earl returned and stood next to a purple lilac bush near the patio. He smiled and said, "I guess my true spirit was released the day of my funeral. My new mission is to remind people to lighten up and not take life so seriously. It all goes by so fast. When we die, we have the opportunity to have fun as we continue to serve others."

"Give us an example," said Betty. She watched Earl as he smiled and adjusted his cap.

"Well, I have a younger son that I visit quite often now. I wish I had spent more time in life having fun with him. He lives alone in the country. At night, while he is asleep, I weed his flower beds and sweep his driveway. During the day, I watch him mow the yard on his green tractor. One of these days, I am going to ride by on his tractor and wave to him. Now THAT will surprise him and make him laugh!"

Later that evening, Elaine, Adele, Betty and Mildred watched Earl place a branch from the lilac bush on each resident's door. Earl rode his motorized scooter like a getaway car so he could escape unnoticed.

The following morning, residents found the purple lilacs Earl had placed on their doors. It was just in time for the official start of summer which would begin in a few days. Betty said, "It's my guess Earl will continue surprising people in the years to come. After getting to know him, I have no doubt Earl will visit those who need a surprise to lift their spirits especially those he loved."

The women returned to the patio and found Earl had left them a purple lilac from the nearby bush. Adele said, "Look, Earl left us a note. She smiled as she read the note out loud.

""To the women of the Patio Club. Please do not report me for stealing lilacs from the nearby bush. My motorized scooter is pretty fast. I doubt anyone will find me.

Signed, Earl.'"

Elaine, Adele, Betty and Mildred laughed at Earl's note. Betty said, "Earl really is a character!

Whenever the women of the Patio Club hear laughter at Happy Visions, they think of Earl. His surprises had a way of touching the hearts of many unsuspecting people.

May your summer be filled with delightful surprises and reminders not to take life too seriously.

With Love from The Patio Club.

The End.

# The Patio Club's Story

IN NOVEMBER OF 2016, I began writing fictional stories for retirement and assisted living communities. This occurred because of a simple request from an older gentleman in his 80s who asked if I could write a story about people "their age." Writing and telling stories has always come easily to me. I happily said , "yes." I was excited at the challenge and have written a story each month since then. They are about a fictional retirement/ assisted living community named *Happy Visions*. Each month I read to retirement and assisted living communities. The joy of doing this is overwhelming.

In July of 2017, I was reading to a group of older women as they sat outside *on the patio* in the shade. The women's ages reached up to 95. When I left the patio that day, I decided at that moment to write a story for them called "The Patio Club." The series began with that story.

The stories I write come effortlessly to me. It is as if I am divinely inspired. As I began writing the first story in the Patio Club series, I was so surprised as I watched the story come to life. It is the story of two sets of sisters, Elaine and Adele from New Jersey, and Mildred and Betty from Kentucky. They made a pact that when they died they would meet up and visit retirement and assisted living communities.

Imagine my surprise—because in real life Elaine and Adele (sisters) were my aunts from New Jersey, and Betty (my mother) and Mildred (my aunt) were sisters from Kentucky! My Aunt Mildred was the last one to join The Patio Club. She passed away earlier in 2017. The Patio Club™ stories now touch people from around the country and hopefully someday from around the world.

My dream is that The Patio Club™ series will be read to the people in assisted living, memory and Hospice care communities. As I read each month to these special people, I realized that it is often difficult to visit loved ones who are in the assisted living population. What I have found is that reading a story seems to transform everyone from the reader to the listener. I have seen people with all kinds of health challenges perk up when listening to the joyful adventures of The Patio Club™. They are in the present moment as they listen and during that time there is nothing wrong with them.

My wish is that people will take the adventure of reading a story (about 12 to 15 minutes) from The Patio Club Series to a loved one. It will transform the visit from one where it may be difficult to find something to talk about, to one where both the reader and listener are moved beyond words.

With gratitude and love,

- Caryn

# Acknowledgments

THE PATIO CLUB is dedicated to my aunts Elaine, Adele, Mildred, and my mother Betty. Although the characters in the Patio Club are fictional, they are based on these important women who impacted my life.

Special thanks to my sons Carson and Cooper, as well as, family and friends who have listened to these stories. They have enthusiastically cheered for me to follow my dream to write and illustrate stories that bring joy and adventure to the lives of others.

Finally, I am grateful to God for the gifts He has given me to serve the people in assisted living, memory and Hospice care.

# About the Author

CARYN BEGAN WRITING children's stories for her children in the 1990s. In 2016, as she read children's stories to assisted living communities, residents asked her to write a story "for people their age." That was how the adventure of writing for the adult and assisted population began.

Since that time, Caryn has written a monthly series called The Patio Club®. It takes place at a retirement home/assisted living community named Happy

Visions. The Patio Club™ are the first stories published by Caryn for that age group. The stories have captured the attention of people of all ages across the country.

The Patio Club™ stories are a bridge between the reader and the listener. Family and friends that visit assisted living, memory and Hospice care communities may struggle for something to talk about. Reading a story like The Patio Club™ to these special residents takes them on an adventure without them ever having to leave the room. It creates an opening for some interesting conversations!

Caryn lives in Colorado. She has two grown sons, Carson and Cooper